Salsa Stories

STORIES AND LINOCUTS BY

Lulu Delacre

SCHOLASTIC PRESS
NEW YORK

Library of Congress Cataloging-in-Publication Data

Delacre, Lulu.
Salsa stories / stories and linocuts by Lulu Delacre.   p.   cm.
Summary: A collection of stories within the story of a family celebration where the guests relate their memories of growing up in various Latin American countries. Also contains recipes.

[1. Latin America Fiction.]   I. Title.   PZ7.D3696Sal   2000   [Fic]—dc21   99-25534   CIP

ISBN 0-590-63118-7

10 9 8 7 6 5 4 3 2 1   00 01 02 03 04

Printed in the U. S. A.
First edition, April 2000

The text type was set in Garamond 3.
The display type was set in Linoscript.
Book design by Marijka Kostiw

Este es sólo para tí,
querida Alicia.

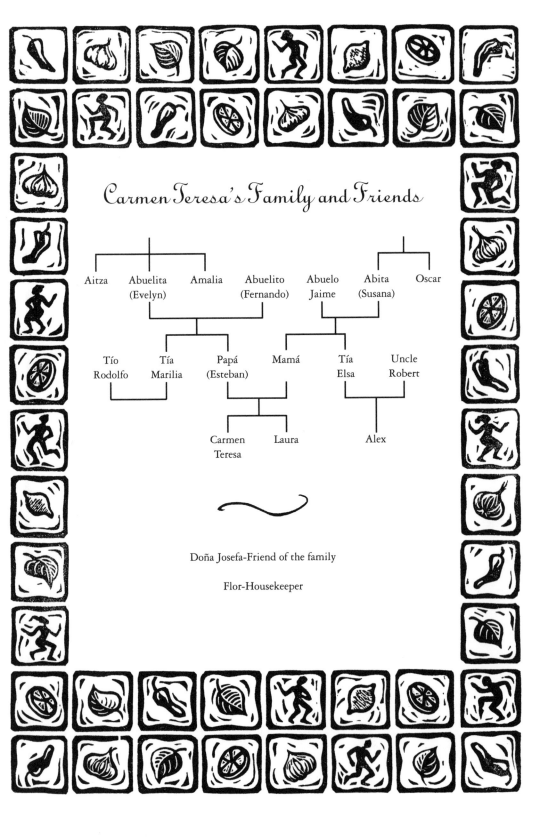

Carmen Teresa's Family and Friends

Aitza — Abuelita (Evelyn) — Amalia — Abuelito (Fernando) — Abuelo Jaime — Abita (Susana) — Oscar

Tío Rodolfo — Tía Marilia — Papá (Esteban) — Mamá — Tía Elsa — Uncle Robert

Carmen Teresa — Laura — Alex

Doña Josefa-Friend of the family

Flor-Housekeeper

New Year's Day

"Esteban! Turn down the stereo," Mamá calls to Papá from the kitchen. She swirls the chicken in its marinade with one hand, then answers the telephone with the other.

Our house stirs with laughter and chatter as guests arrive, one by one. The cousins run noisily about our basement to the beat of salsa music that blares from speakers on two floors. In the dining room, Abuelito, Abuelo Jaime, Uncle Robert, and Papá click dominoes together, concentrating on each move of their game. They play with Abuelito's lucky dominoes, the ones he brought with him from Cuba forty years ago.

In the kitchen, my grandma Abita, our housekeeper Flor, and I rhythmically chop and slice. The rich, pungent scent of garlic crackling in olive oil rises from the stove. We are helping Mamá prepare the *sofrito* sauce for her *arroz con pollo*. This is the rice dish for which Mamá is famous among all our friends and family.

Flor and Abita chatter away in Spanish, as they

struggle to hold back tears from the chopped onion. Flor tells Abita about the trip she will soon make to Guatemala for Holy Week.

"I've been saving for over a year to visit my family," she says. Flor has saved not only for her ticket, but also for the gifts she will bring to everyone from America: new jeans, walkie-talkies, a small TV, and the latest toys.

Abita nods her approval.

Above the din of music, children's shouts, and clattering pots and pans, we miraculously hear the doorbell.

"Carmen Teresa, get the door!" my little sister Laura calls from the basement stairs.

"You get it — please!" I shout back. "I'm busy." I'm afraid that if I abandon my spot in the kitchen, I will lose it to someone else who is anxious to help. I love to cook, and when company comes, a good spot in Mamá's kitchen is hard to come by.

I watch Laura dash to open the door.

"Doña Josefa!" she calls out, then flies into the old woman's open arms.

"*Feliz año nuevo, Laurita,*" Doña Josefa says, as she gives Laura a warm hug and a present. Doña Josefa is from Peru. She is one of the doctors from the free clinic where Mamá volunteers. Mamá always says Doña Josefa loves to dote on us since she has no children of her own.

Laura thanks her for the gift, then steals into the dining room to open it.

Doña Josefa finds me in the kitchen. She is holding a package wrapped in brown paper. Her leathery hands are a shade darker than the wrapping. She's about to place the package into my open hands, but stops herself when she notices they are covered in cilantro. She takes the package back to the entrance and puts it on a small table instead.

"For after you clean your hands, Carmen Teresa," she says.

The last to arrive are Tía Marilia and Tío Rodolfo. They've brought bottles of *coquito* and the latest hits from Rubén Blades and Willie Colón.

"Would you believe this?" Tía Marilia jokes, glancing at the guests. "All the men are enjoying themselves while the women slave in the kitchen. There are some old customs that not even life in the States can change!"

Tía Marilia is my favorite aunt. She has such a quick wit, and when she is around, there is laughter everywhere.

Suddenly, my sister tugs at my sleeve.

"Look, Carmen, look what I got!" Laura shows me a beautiful cloth doll that Doña Josefa gave her. "Let me see yours, what did you get?"

Curious to find out, I wash my hands and look for my gift. But it is not on the table where Doña Josefa left it. And no one is near the table except our little cousin Alex. When Laura sees him, she eagerly takes his hand and tries to play with him. But Alex has just learned to walk and he prefers to gleefully charge around the house.

"Laura!" calls Abuelita. "The cinnamon!"

Laura quickly forgets about Alex and my gift and runs to do her only and favorite job in the kitchen. She must sprinkle cinnamon over the cool *natilla*. Abuelita prepared the velvety cream for dessert and filled twenty-five small bowls with it. This dessert is Laura's favorite, and after carefully studying each bowl, she mischievously covers the fullest one with a blanket of the spice. That's her way of claiming it.

Mamá calls everyone to eat. We've set the platters on the kitchen counter and people stream in to serve themselves. Then they sit wherever they please at the dining room table, at the kitchen table, or in the living room.

Abuelito stands up to say grace. He can sometimes go on for quite a long time, for he loves to be the center of attention. And he always ends his prayer with the same old Spanish saying: "*¡Salud, dinero, amor, y tiempo para disfrutarlos!* Health, money, love, and time to enjoy it all!" he says. Everyone is very hungry by the time he finally gets to this part.

I take a huge mouthful of steaming *yuca* when Doña Josefa sits next to me.

"Did you like your gift?" she asks.

I quickly swallow and excuse myself to avoid the embarrassing situation of having to tell her I've misplaced it.

I look again on the entrance table and under it, but the package is gone. In whispers, I ask my parents and some relatives if they have seen it, but no one has. To avoid Doña Josefa, I duck into the kitchen where I find Tía Marilia and Tío Rodolfo. They've been lured to the center of the kitchen floor by the dance music that's become irresistible to them. Gracefully they twirl into each other's arms and show off their fiery moves. Inspired by her sister-in-law, Mamá pulls me to "the dance floor" to teach me some basic salsa steps. Reluctantly, I follow.

"Don't look at your feet," warns Mamá. "Just feel the rhythm of the music."

Across the room, I spot Laura next to Alex. I abandon the dance lesson to find out if she has seen my missing gift. Before I can ask, Alex topples the little rooster that was perched on the hand-carved nativity scene. And while Laura carefully rearranges the pieces, Alex has moved on to playing with something else. I peer over his shoulder to find he's trying to unwrap a brown package. *It's my gift!*

"Oh, Alex," I say. "Let me help you with that."

I let him unwrap the small parcel, then give him the wrapping paper to play with. He seems quite happy to noisily rustle and crinkle the paper.

My gift from Doña Josefa is a book filled with blank pages and covered with a red fabric sprinkled with daisies. Inside I find an inscription:

Dear Carmen Teresa,
When I was your age, I kept a journal in a book just like this one. I hope you'll find a treasured use for yours, as I did for mine.

Doña Josefa

"Show me!" demands Laura. A smug look comes over her face when she sees the book. She is pleased that it is not something she likes better than her doll.

Relieved to have found the gift, I run to Doña Josefa to thank her.

"What should I write in this book?" I ask her.

Doña Josefa's creased face lights up with her smile. "There are many things you can write," she says. "Perhaps you will want to keep a journal, like I did."

"Or," offers Abuelita, "you could write about things that have happened to you when you were younger."

"Yes. Or maybe, you could collect stories from our family and friends," suggests Mamá, "since everyone is here today."

"Stories — *ahh, ¡cuentos!*" calls Abuelito from his seat at the dining room table where he has been eavesdropping. "I have a great story for your book, Carmen Teresa. But first," he says in his deep voice, "Abuelita, bring me more of that wonderful *arroz con pollo,* please."

Abuelita nods to Flor, who quickly refills his plate.

Abuelito glows as everyone gathers around him to hear his tale.

"When you are finished, Señor," Flor adds, "I have a story for Carmen Teresa, too."

"*¡Ah! No, no, damas primero,*" says Abuelito. "Ladies first."

"Always a gentleman," replies Doña Josefa. "And who knows, maybe we'll all take a turn. Why don't you start, Flor?" As soon as we are comfortably settled around the dining room table, Flor begins her story.

A Carpet for Holy Week
FLOR'S STORY

Ever since I was a little girl in Guatemala City, my family has made an *alfombra* for Holy Week. *Alfombras* are beautiful carpets handmade from colored sawdust and fresh flowers. Every Palm Sunday morning, we make an *alfombra* on the street right in front of our house. That week, dozens of processions walk by. Porters, who carry splendid statues of Jesus and Mary, follow the pathways of beautiful carpets that are spread throughout the neighborhood. We wait for one that will cross our carpet. At last it comes! And for us, it is like the Lord Himself has walked upon our carpet.

One Friday during Lent, when I was twelve, we had just finished Mamá's *bacalao a la vizcaína,* her delicious codfish stew, when Abuelo Marco asked me to do something I had only dreamed of doing.

"Flor," he said, smoothing his mustache that was now the color of his weathered straw hat. "Since you are the oldest grandchild, how would you like to make the design for the carpet this year?"

"Oh, Abuelo!" I shouted joyfully. Ever since I could walk, I had helped him with the carpet. When I was very young, I was only allowed to stamp on the sawdust. Later, I was allowed to help dye it. And for the past few years, I carefully sifted out what was needed for its colorful border. But I had never had the honor of making the design. I couldn't wait to look through our well-worn collection of wooden stencils and pull out the ones I liked best.

I could feel the expectant stares of Abuelo, my parents, and my three little brothers as I sat on my chair, thinking. I had seen how Abuelo lovingly created new carpet designs by mixing patterns. I tried to remember sawdust carpets I had seen before and the many border stencils I knew we had stored. Then, I decided just what I wanted to do. I took some paper and a pencil, and started to draw. Abuelo Marco nodded in approval when I was finished.

"I think we'll have a beautiful carpet, Flor," he said.

The following day, Papá and all three of my brothers drove to the sawmill to get the sawdust. The owner of the sawmill gave away most of his sawdust just for making carpets for Holy Week. When Papá returned with twenty large sacks, we all helped carry them into the house. For the next several hours my mother and I stirred the sawdust in big vats of dye. We made batches of red, white, green, and black. The last thing I did that afternoon was to trace the new flying dove pattern on plywood. Papá cut out the stencil. I could already imagine the dove in the middle of a golden background surrounded by borders of flowers and geometric shapes.

By Thursday, we had everything ready to make the carpet. And on Palm Sunday at dawn we would assemble it right in front of our house. I couldn't wait.

But then something terrible happened.

When I woke up Saturday morning, the house was in chaos.

"You stay here!" I heard Papá shout. "I'll go see what happened!"

He ran out the door, leaving Mamá watching anxiously by the window. Doña Paca, our next-door neighbor, had heard the turmoil, and rushed over to help with my younger brothers. She was in the kitchen feeding them *torrejas.* They were too young to understand what was going on, but the syrupy warm bread kept them out of the way.

"Mamá, ¿qué pasa?" I asked sleepily. "What's going on?"

"*Ay,* Flor," Mamá wept softly as she put her rosary down. "It's Abuelo Marco," she said. "There's a fire in his apartment. Your father has gone to help."

While Mamá dragged herself to the sofa to continue her prayer, I ran to the window and threw the shutters open wide. Between the modern signs projecting from storefronts and the cascade of ferns hanging from the balcony next door, I could see a crowd gathering at the entrance of Abuelo Marco's building. A cloud of black smoke was escaping from his window and rising to the sky. Frozen in place, I bit my fingernails, my eyes fixed on the crowd. What if something bad had happened to Abuelo?

"Is Abuelo inside his apartment?" I asked Mamá. "Did you try to call him?" But Mamá was deep in prayer and did not hear me. Soothed by her repetitive Hail Marys, I continued to look for Abuelo. I even made up prayers of my own.

The sun outside was blinding and I squinted my eyes to see clearly. The firefighters were opening a path through the crowd. It was then that I saw Papá coming out of Abuelo's building. And a moment later Abuelo appeared by his side.

"Mamá! Mamá! Abuelo is alright!" I cried out.

"*Ay, Santo Dios,*" Mamá sighed, kissing the cross of her rosary.

Soon Papá returned home with Abuelo. We greeted them with hugs and strong coffee. For the next few hours, the phone didn't stop ringing. A stream of neighbors, family, and friends came in to see how Abuelo was doing. All the while I helped by entertaining my brothers.

Nobody mentioned the carpet at all that afternoon, and I began to worry that we weren't going to assemble it tomorrow. It was difficult to hide my disappointment. It was difficult to hide how eager I was for Abuelo see how my first *alfombra* would turn out.

When the commotion finally died down, my grandfather took a long nap. Afterward he came into the living room, followed by Mamá and Papá. Holding onto his cane, he sank onto the checkered couch and gathered his grandchildren near him.

"Well, it looks like I'll be staying here with you for a while," Abuelo said, with a weary look on his face. "Everything inside my apartment is charred or burnt to ashes. But it doesn't matter. Who wants all those ancient things anyway?"

For a long moment nobody said anything. I thought it was unfair that he had lost everything — his old books and photographs, his furniture-making tools, and even his favorite rocking chair — all was gone. I couldn't imagine what it would be like to lose all my favorite things.

"The only thing that matters is that you are alive." Mamá finally broke the silence. "We'll love to have you here with us."

We all hugged him together.

"Abuelo," I asked, "is there something I can do?"

"*Nada,* Florcita," Abuelo smiled. "Not a thing." But after a pause he asked, "Do we have everything ready for tomorrow's carpet?"

"This is not a time to think about making an *alfombra,*" complained Mamá. "There are other more important things to take care of."

Fortunately, Abuelo Marco would not hear of any excuses. He was not about to break a tradition that he had loved since he was a little boy. Not for a fire — not for anything. So we all agreed we would make the carpet tomorrow as we had planned.

The following morning, my family was outside at the crack of dawn. My uncles opened sacks of sawdust and poured their contents inside a wooden frame. Amidst shrieks of delight, my three little brothers spread, stomped, and leveled the thick, golden foundation on which the design would be placed. Then, my

mother and I brought out big bowls of the dyed, moist sawdust we had prepared a few days before. Layer by layer, hour after hour, we sifted each color into the wooden stencils, taking pains not to step in what had already been made. Abuelo Marco sat on a chair nearby, watching as we worked. On the next street, several families worked on a two-block-long carpet they had been making since the night before.

Just as we finished, the bells of La Merced Church chimed loudly. Abuelo had gone inside to rest. It was then that I lovingly sifted something new into the carpet. Mamá came out and handed me a glass of cold *horchata*. Its bittersweet taste reflected my feelings. I drank it while we admired our work on the pavement.

"I like what you added to the design, Flor," said Mamá. "And I know Abuelo will like it, too."

After the fire, I had wanted to do something for Abuelo. So during the night I had cut two new stencils out of cardboard. One was the silhouette of an old man, the other was that of a flame.

A crowd of people gathered around us as we put the finishing touches on our *alfombra*. Papá sprayed the sawdust carpet with water once again, to protect it from the wind. Then he removed the wooden frame. The carpet's brilliant colors glowed in the morning sun.

Abuelo came out. As the sound of the tuba grew

louder, we knew the procession was coming near. Two long lines of men dressed in purple tunics carried an immense wooden platform on their shoulders. On it stood a statue of Jesus. Behind them, two lines of shawled women carried a platform with a statue of Mary. Burdened by the weight, the porters swayed from side to side as they solemnly walked forward.

Mamá, Papá, Abuelo, my brothers, and I gathered around our carpet and joined hands. I stood next to Abuelo, and I wondered if he liked what I had done.

"*Los cucuruchos,* the porters, they're coming!" said Abuelo, his voice filled with excitement. "They will finally step on the most beautiful *alfombra* our family has ever made."

A warm sensation deep inside me began to spread through my body like the sweet oozing syrup that soaked the *torrejas.* I felt the heat rise through my ears and color my cheeks. I watched as the porters first admired my design, and then slowly advanced across the carpet. They stepped on the green-and-white geometrical border. They stepped on the red-and-white flowered border. They stepped on the golden background where the white dove carried the black silhouette of an old man away from the red-and-yellow flames below it. Finally, they stepped on the two words I had written in black letters.

When the fragile carpet had vanished under the feet of the worshippers, I felt Abuelo squeeze my hand, and I looked up to meet his gaze. He had a broad smile on his face. It was then that I fully understood the importance of the words that I had written with black sawdust. *Gracias, Señor.*

Thank you, Lord.

Amen.

At the Beach
ABUELITO'S STORY

$\mathcal{I}$ remember those evenings well when I was a young boy in Cuba, those balmy island nights before a trip to Guanabo Beach. The spicy aroma of *tortilla española* that Mami had left to cool would waft through the house as I lay in my bed. But I was always too excited to sleep. All I could think about was the soft white sand, the warm foamy water, and Mami's delicious *tortilla.* Ahhh. A day at the beach. It was full of possibilities.

One Saturday in May, I was awakened at the crack of dawn by sounds of laughter. My aunts, Rosa and Olga, had arrived with hammocks, blankets, and an iron kettle filled with Aunt Rosa's steaming *congrí.* And best of all, they had arrived with my cousins: Luisa, Mari, and little Javi. Uncle Toni had come, too.

When we were ready to leave, Papi, the only one in the family who owned a car, packed his Ford woody wagon with the nine of us. No one cared that we children had to squeeze into the back along with the clutter of pots and plates, food and bags, towels and blankets and hammocks. Soon the engine turned, and the car rumbled down the road into the rising sun.

Along the way, we drove past sugarcane fields and roadside markets. My cousins and I shouted warnings to the barking dogs and laughed at the frightened hens that scurried in every direction at the sight of our car. It seemed like a long time until the cool morning breeze that blew into the windows turned warm. And the growing heat made the aroma of Mami's *tortilla* all the more tempting.

"Lick your skin, Fernando," my older cousin Luisa told me. "If it tastes salty, that means we'll be there any time now."

She was right. My skin tasted salty. And soon — almost magically — the turquoise ocean appeared as we rounded a bend in the road. Papi pulled into the familiar dirt lot and parked under the pine trees. While the grown-ups unloaded the car, we eagerly jumped out and ran toward the sea, peeling off our clothes along the way.

"Remember, don't go too far!" Mami and Aunt Olga warned us sternly from the distance. I turned to see them picking up our scattered clothing.

When we reached the edge of the ocean, the water

felt cold. I waded farther in and went under to warm up quickly. When I emerged I saw Luisa, Mari, and little Javi, all standing still in the clear water. They were watching the schools of tiny gold-and-black striped fish rush between their legs. Then they swam over to join me and together we rode the big waves.

Later, Uncle Toni came in to play shark with us. We splashed, and swallowed the stinging sea water as he chased us above and under the waves. But after a while, we tired him out, and he went back to sit with the grown-ups.

I was getting very hungry, and for a moment I thought of returning with him to sneak a bite of Mami's *tortilla*. But then I had a better idea.

"Let's explore the reef!" I said.

"*¡Sí!*" everyone agreed. "Let's go!"

We all splashed out of the water and ran, dripping wet, across the sand. High above, the sun beat down on us.

When we got to the marbled rocks, Luisa looked concerned. "Our moms told us not to come this far," she said.

"I know the way well," I replied. "Besides, nobody will notice. They're too busy talking."

I looked in the distance and saw Mami and my two aunts in the shady spot they had picked. They had set

up a nice camp. The hammocks were tied to the pine trees, the blankets were spread over the fine sand. Papi and Uncle Toni played dominoes, while they sipped coffee and shared the *cucurucho de maní* they had purchased from the peanut vendor. They were having fun. No one would miss us for a long time.

"Watch out for sea urchins!" I warned as I led the group on our climb. The spiny black sea urchins hid inside the crevices and crannies of the rough boulders. It was very painful if you stepped on one. Luisa and Mari followed behind me. They were careful to only step on the rocks I stepped on. Little Javi came last. He stopped constantly to look at the *cobitos,* the tiny hermit crabs that scurried around on the rocks, and at the iridescent tropical fish that were concealed in the deepest tide pools. I had to keep checking behind me to make sure he didn't stray from our path.

Just then, I turned around to watch helplessly as Javi slipped on an algae-covered rock. "*¡Cuidado!*" I warned. But it was too late.

"*¡Ay!*" he shrieked, and then began to cry uncontrollably.

Cautiously, we all hurried back to help Javi. Luisa and Mari crouched down to examine his foot.

"He stepped on a sea urchin!" Mari cried. "Now what are we going to do?"

"We should have never followed you," Luisa lamented. "We'll all be punished."

At that moment I did not want to think of what the punishment would be. What if we couldn't have any of Mami's *tortilla*? All I knew was that we had to help Javi right away. I looked around and found a piece of drift-wood.

"Luisa," I ordered. "Hold his leg still while I remove the urchin from his foot."

Luisa held Javi's leg still as Mari held his hand and tried to comfort him. But Javi's desperate cries were now drowning out the sound of the sea.

I pulled and tugged, but the urchin wouldn't budge. It was stuck to Javi's foot by the tips of its spines. Javi was scared and in pain. And we were too far from our parents to ask for help. What if we couldn't get Javi back? I struggled relentlessly until I was finally able to remove the spiny creature from his foot.

Gently, Luisa poured some sea water over Javi's foot. That was when she noticed there was still a piece of the sea urchin's spine lodged in it. Javi wasn't going to be able to walk back and he was much too heavy for us to carry. We had to remove that piece of spine so that he could walk on his own.

The sun burnt our backs as we all took turns trying to dislodge the sea urchin's spine.

"I have an idea," said Luisa suddenly. She removed her hair barrettes and held them like tweezers. Then, with the smallest movement, she pulled the broken spine out. With that solved, we started back.

I helped Javi walk on his sore foot. He wept and limped with every step. Our walk back seemed endless. As we got closer I realized that we would have to explain how it was that we went to the reef in the first place. I would surely end up with no *tortilla* if we told the truth.

"What will we do now?" Mari asked.

"We'll have to tell our parents what happened," said Luisa matter-of-factly.

"No!" I said emphatically. "We'll be punished for sure."

We walked the rest of the way in silence. The sound of crashing waves, children playing, and seagulls' calls became a background drone to Javi's cries.

When we finally reached our parents, Javi was crying louder than ever. Aunt Olga took one look at him and gasped. "*¡Niños!* Children! What's happened to Javi?"

Mari looked at Luisa. Luisa looked at me. Javi cried even louder.

"Well . . . ," I hesitated. By now everyone was staring at me. "We were walking along the beach looking for cockles and urchin shells," I began, "when I found a live sea urchin attached to a piece of driftwood. So I called the others. Javi came running so fast that he stepped on it by accident."

Luisa and Mari stared at me in disbelief. I didn't think they liked my story.

"Let me see your foot, Javi," Aunt Olga said, kneeling next to her son.

Mami and Aunt Rosa looked on as Aunt Olga examined Javi's foot closely. Then she gave him a big hug and a kiss. "He's fine," she said at last. "It looks like the children were able to pull it out."

And at this good news, Javi's tears disappeared and were replaced by a big broad smile. "I'm hungry," he said.

"Then let's have lunch," Aunt Olga suggested.

I was dumbfounded. Not only had they believed me, but we were also going to eat Mami's *tortilla*!

The men went back to their domino game. The women went back to their conversation as they busied themselves serving everybody. No one but me seemed to notice how quiet Luisa and Mari had grown.

Mami handed me a plate filled with my favorite foods. The *tortilla* smelled delicious. But I was unable to eat. I looked up at Luisa and Mari who were quietly picking at their food. I watched Mami as she served herself and sat next to my aunts. I looked at my plate again. How could I enjoy my food when I knew I had done something I wasn't supposed to do? There was only one thing I could do now. I stood up, picked up my plate, and went right over to Mami.

"What's wrong, Fernando?" Mami asked.

I looked back at Luisa and Mari and swallowed hard. Then, I handed Mami my untouched plate.

"You wouldn't have given me this if I had told you the truth," I said.

Mami looked puzzled. The whole group grew silent and watched me struggle. I was very embarrassed.

"It was my fault," Luisa said. "I should have stopped them."

"And I went along," said Mari.

"No, no, it was my idea to go to the reef," I said. Then I told everyone about our adventure at the reef. When I was finished, Mami looked at me with tear-filled eyes.

"You are right, Fernando," she said. "I should punish you for doing something you knew not to do. Some-body could have been seriously hurt."

"I know," I whispered, "and I'm sorry." But then the

glimmer of a smile softened Mami's expression. She slid her arm over my shoulders as she said, "You know, Fernando, anyone can make mistakes. But not everyone has the courage to admit it. *Gracias.* Thank you for telling the truth."

That afternoon, under the shade of the pine trees, the nine of us sat down on the old blankets for lunch. We had *congrí,* bread, and Mami's famous *tortilla española.* And do you know something? That day it tasted better than it ever had before.

The Night of San Juan
ABUELITA'S STORY

Back in the 1940s, in Puerto Rico's walled city of Old San Juan, everybody knew everybody else. We neighborhood children played freely together on the narrow streets, while from windows and balconies adults kept a watchful eye on us. It was only my lonely friend José Manuel who was forbidden from joining us.

"Look, Evelyn," whispered Amalia. "He's up there again, watching us play."

Aitza and I looked up. There he was, sitting on his balcony floor. He peered sadly down at us through the wrought iron railing, while his grandma's soap opera blared from the radio inside. No matter how hard José Manuel tried, he could not convince his grandma to let him play out on the street.

"Too many crazy drivers! Too hard, the cobblestones! *¡Muy peligroso!*" His grandma would shake her head and say, "Too dangerous!"

Besides her fear of danger on the street, José Manuel's grandma kept to herself and never smiled, so most of us were afraid of her. That is, until my sisters and I changed all that.

"One day," Amalia suddenly announced, "I'm going to ask his grandma to let him come down and play." If anyone would have the courage to do that, it was my little sister Amalia. Even though she was only seven, she was also the most daring of the three of us.

We never knew what she would do next. In fact, at that very moment I could see a mischievous grin spreading across her freckled face as two elegant women turned the corner of Calle Sol. Once they strolled down the street in front of us, Amalia swiftly snuck up behind them and flipped their skirts up to expose their lace-trimmed slips.

"*¡Sinvergüenza!*" the women cried out. "Little rascal!"

We could hardly hold our laughter in. We all looked up to make sure none of the neighbors had seen her. If anyone had, we would surely have been scolded as soon as we got home. News traveled fast in our neighborhood.

Luckily, only José Manuel was watching us with amusement in his wistful eyes. Grateful for an audience, Amalia smiled at him, curtsied, and ran down the street toward the old cathedral with us chasing after her. I couldn't help but feel sorry for my friend as we left him behind.

There was hardly any sea breeze that day, and running in the humidity made us quite hot.

"Let's get some coconut sherbet," said Amalia, peeling her damp red curls away from her sweaty neck.

"*¡Sí, sí!*" we agreed, and we chattered excitedly about our plans for that night all the way to the ice-cream vendor's wooden cart by the harbor.

It was June twenty-third, and that night was the Night of San Juan. For this holiday, the tradition was to go to the beach, and at exactly midnight, everyone would walk backward into the sea. People say that doing this three times on the Night of San Juan brings good luck. I thought of my friend José Manuel. Perhaps if he did this with us, his luck would change, and his grandma would allow him to play with us outside on the street.

I thought about this as we bought our coconut sherbet and then ate it perched on the knobby roots of the ancient tree above the port. Excitement stirred in me while the distant ships disappeared over the horizon.

"How can we get José Manuel to go to the beach tonight?" I asked my sisters.

"Evelyn, you know very well his grandma will never let him go," Aitza said. "You know what she will say —"

"*¡Muy peligroso!*" Aitza and Amalia teased at once. "Too dangerous!"

It was getting close to dinnertime, and we knew we had to be home soon if we wanted our parents to take us to the beach that night. So we took the shortcut back across the main square. In the plaza, groups of men played dominoes while the women sat by the fountain and gossiped. Back on the street we heard the vegetable vendor chanting:

"*¡Vendo yuca, plátanos, tomates!*"

He came around every evening to sell his fresh cassava, plantains, tomatoes, and other fruits and vegetables.

Leaning from her balcony, a big woman lowered a basket that was tied by a cord to the rail. In it was the money that the vendor replaced with two green plantains. As we approached our street I saw José Manuel and his grandma out on the second floor. She gave José Manuel money and went back inside. He was about to lower his basket when I had an idea. Maybe there was a way we could ask him to join us.

"What if we send José Manuel a note in his grandma's basket inviting him to go to the beach with us tonight?" I offered.

"It will never work," Aitza said. "His grandma will not like it. We could get into trouble."

"Then we could ask her personally," I said.

"But what excuse could we use to go up there?" said Aitza. "Nobody ever shows up uninvited at José Manuel's house."

"Wait! I know what we can do," Amalia said, jumping up and down. "We'll tell him to drop something. Then we'll go up to return it."

Even though Aitza was very reluctant, we convinced her to try our plan. We wrote the note and asked the vegetable vendor to please place it in José Manuel's basket next to the vegetables. We impatiently waited on the corner as we watched. When he opened the note, he looked puzzled. He took the tomatoes he had purchased in to his grandmother. Soon he returned with his little red ball. He had just sat down to play when suddenly the ball fell from the balcony. It bounced several times, rolled down the hill, and bumped into a wall. Amalia flew after it. "I got it!" she called triumphantly, offering me her find.

With José Manuel's ball in my hand we climbed up the worn stairs of his pink apartment house. And while Aitza and I stood nervously outside his apartment trying to catch our breath, Amalia knocked loudly on the wooden door. With a squeaking sound it slowly opened, and there stood José Manuel's grandma wearing a frown as grim as her black widow's dress.

"*¿Sí?*" she said. "How can I help you?"

Aitza and I looked at each other. She looked as afraid as I felt. But without hesitation, Amalia took the little ball from my hand and proudly showed it to José Manuel's grandma. I wanted to run, but a glimpse of José Manuel's hopeful expression made me stay.

"This belongs to José Manuel," Amalia declared. "We came to return it." Amalia took a deep breath, then took a step forward. "We also wanted to know if he could come to the beach tonight with our family."

Aitza and I meekly stood behind Amalia.

"The beach?" José Manuel's grandma asked, surprised, as she took the little ball from Amalia's palm.

"Y-y-yes," I stuttered. "Tonight is the Night of San Juan, and our parents take us to the beach every year."

José Manuel's grandma scowled at us. How silly to think she would ever let him go. I suddenly felt embarrassed and turned to leave, pulling both sisters with me by their arms.

"Wait," we heard her raspy voice behind us. "Come inside for a *surullito de maíz.*"

It was then that I smelled the aroma of the corn fritters that was escaping from the kitchen. José Manuel's grandma was making *surullitos* for dinner.

"Oh, yes!" Amalia followed her in without a thought. And before we knew it, we were all seated in the living room rocking chairs next to José Manuel, eating the most delicious corn fritters that we dipped in garlicky sauce. Somehow, sitting there with José Manuel, his grandma seemed less scary. After we finished, José Manuel's grandma thanked us for our invitation and said she would let us know.

José Manuel smiled.

When we got home we found Mami waiting with her hands on her hips. She had just hung up the phone with José Manuel's grandma. She had reason to be upset. Not only were we late for supper, but in our excitement we had forgotten to ask for permission before inviting José Manuel to the beach. We all looked down, not knowing what to do or say.

"It wasn't my fault. It was Evelyn and Amalia's idea," volunteered Aitza, the coward.

"*Bendito,* Mami," I said. "Don't punish us, we forgot."

"Forgot?" Mami asked.

"*Sí,* Mami," we all said at once. "We are sorry."

"Actually it was very nice of you girls to invite him,"

said Mami. "But please remember to ask me first next time."

Late that night the whole family went to the beach as was our tradition on the Night of San Juan. But this time was special, for we had José Manuel with us.

The full moon shone against the velvet sky. The tide was high, and the beach swarmed with young revelers who, like us, had waited all year for this night's irresistible dip in the dark ocean. The moment we reached the water we all turned around, held hands, and jumped backward into the rushing waves. Amalia stumbled forward, Aitza joyfully splashed back, and so did I as I let go of my sister's hand. But my other hand remained tightly clasped to José Manuel's. When my friend and I took our third plunge into the sea, I wished good luck would come to him, and that from then on, his grandma would allow him to play with us out on the street. And as a wave lifted us high in the water, I suddenly knew this wish would come true.

Teatime

ABITA'S STORY

I used to be a sickly child those years long ago in Buenos Aires. Once I had a severe virus that left me unable to eat or drink any dairy foods for eighty-nine days. Eighty-nine long days. I know because I counted each one carefully on my calendar. And I couldn't have been more pleased the day my doctor assured me that I could have milk again. That meant that at teatime that afternoon I would be able to have *alfajores.* Those were my favorite sandwich cookies, the kind that were filled with milk caramel. All day at school I thought of nothing else, and couldn't wait to get home.

Finally, the dismissal bell rang loudly and snapped me out of my sweet daydream. I leaped up from my seat, and put on my blue wool coat and matching beret and gloves to protect me from the chilly weather. Buenos Aires is always chilly in July. For while half of the world is warmed by the summer sun, Argentina is gliding through winter.

"See you Monday, Susana!" I heard my schoolmates

call from behind me as I crossed the courtyard. I barely had time to turn around and wave good-bye to them before I cut into the wind and hurried home to my mother and Abuela Elena. Our apartment house was only two blocks away from school, but the more I rushed to get there, the further away it seemed. I was trying to get home before my twin brother, Oscar, even though I knew he would run home ahead of me. That way he could sneak into the kitchen and take inventory of the afternoon sweets. At eleven years old, I might have been taller — but he was, without a doubt, faster. Particularly when sweets were involved.

Today's afternoon tea, *la hora del té*, was a special one. Aunt Cecilia and Aunt Morena were coming to join us. Of course, teatime was delicious every day of the week. But it was especially delicious when we had company. Only then would Abuela Elena buy *alfajores de dulce de leche*. And today, after eighty-nine days of deprivation, I would finally satisfy my craving. My mouth watered at the thought.

"Hola, querida," Abuela Elena greeted me, then took my coat and hung it next to Oscar's. He had, as I'd predicted, arrived before me. I washed my hands quickly and went to kiss my parents and aunts who had just sat down at the elegantly set table. After I took my place

next to Aunt Morena, Elvira appeared in her starched white cap and apron through the kitchen door, with a steaming silver pot of English tea.

"Leave it on the tea cart next to me, Elvira," said Mamá.

As soon as Elvira went back into the kitchen, Mamá prepared each individual cup with experienced grace. I saw her lace the perfumed tea with thin ribbons of cold milk and spoonfuls of sugar while I craned my neck to peek at the plate of sweets behind the centerpiece. But the large bouquet of roses hid them well.

Mamá served the tea to Oscar and me last. Then, as always, she passed the plate of tea sandwiches around. After that, she passed around a plate filled with buttered toast. And when everyone had their fill of tea sandwiches and toast, it was finally time for the sweets.

As Mamá lifted the serving dish with tiny brioches and sweet scones, I saw the unimaginable. I looked again in case I had seen it wrong. But I had not. In the middle of the sweets plate there was only one *alfajor!* Aunt Cecilia took the dish, chose a scone, and ceremoniously passed it on to Abuela who served herself a brioche. Neither of them touched the lone sandwich cookie. I could not take my eyes off of it. Papá took a

scone and handed me the rest. As I held the plate in my hands, time seemed to stop. My whole body ached for that *alfajor.* But one look at Mamá and it was clear I had no choice. Her silent gaze firmly warned me against improper manners at the table. I knew exactly what she was thinking: *Guests come first.* So reluctantly, I handed the plate to Aunt Morena. I knew she had a sweet tooth as big as mine, and I expected her to take what I had dreamed of eating for so long. But she didn't. Then, the plate had barely reached Oscar when the worst possible thing happened. With a single quick movement of his hand and a sneaky smile, Oscar raised the cookie to his lips — and gobbled it up!

I gave Mamá a stricken look.

"Elvira," Mamá called behind her. "Bring more *alfajores, por favor.*"

But when Elvira returned from the kitchen, she was empty-handed. "Señora," she whispered, "there are none left."

I stared, dumbfounded.

"What?" asked Mamá. "Did you not buy half a dozen?"

"We bought the last four at the bakery," said Abuela.

"That means there are three left!" I blurted out.

"They've disappeared, Niña Susana," Elvira apologized. "I looked everywhere in the kitchen and couldn't find them."

"I wonder what could have happened to them," Abuela mused.

Oscar, who had been quietly savoring the last bit of milk-caramel cookie, started to cough. He coughed until Abuela excused him and led him to his room. It looked fake to me. I figured he wanted to get away for some reason. But why? Abuela came in through the hallway and instantly disappeared into the kitchen.

My aunts kept talking with my father, as though nothing had happened. But I knew something interesting was going on behind the closed kitchen door. I had to find out what it was, so I excused myself and followed Abuela.

Abuela Elena was in front of the pantry sifting through bottles, cans, and boxes. As she was about to remove a pile of table linen, a small paper package from the bakery appeared in the corner of the shelf. It had a tear in it, and *alfajor* crumbs lay all around it.

"*¡Qué mala pata!*" exclaimed Elvira with a clap of her hands. "What bad luck!" She proceeded to pick up the torn package.

"What happened?" I asked.

"Your brother secretly ate two *alfajores* and hid the third one for later," said Abuela Elena, motioning to Elvira to throw away the package and its contents.

"And a mouse got to it before he did!" Elvira sighed as she wiped the shelf with a soapy rag. "It's too late to buy any more this evening."

I stood there frozen as I watched Elvira clear away all the crumbs from the precious *alfajor* and throw them into the garbage. The rage bubbling inside me soon gave way to numb disbelief. Abuela Elena tenderly took my hand and led me back into the dining room. With my well-learned good manners, I forced a smile and sat down to tea again.

The next morning at breakfast, I found Oscar's seat empty. Abuela told me he had been up all night with indigestion. In the early hours of the day he was quite weak. But as time went by he became hungry once again, and that meant he felt much better. That is, until Mamá told him that for the next eighty-nine days, whenever we had guests for tea, I was to have *his* share of *alfajores* — as well as mine.

Birthday Piñata

UNCLE ROBERT'S STORY

One bright clear morning, right before my eighth birthday, Mami took me to my grandma Rosa's, just as she did every morning on her way to work.

"*Apúrate, m'ijo,*" said Mami. "Hurry, or I'll miss my ride!"

Leaving a trail of red dust behind us, I ran to keep up with her as she pulled me along the narrow streets of our *barrio,* in the Mexican town of Juárez. Neighbors who trickled out of their houses to start their daily routines greeted us as we passed. But there was no time to stop and talk. Small pearls of sweat rose on Mami's brow and rolled down her carefully made-up face as we rushed along.

Today, as always, Mami had put on a freshly ironed dress, curled her light brown hair, and slipped her old plastic sandals onto her feet. She didn't want to ruin her high heels. So she would put them on just before she reached the Texas border.

When we finally arrived at Mama Rosa's, Mami

quickly bent down and offered me her cheek. *"Dame un beso,* Roberto, give me a kiss," she said, smoothing back my hair with her hand. "I get paid today. So when I pick you up we'll go to the market to buy the *piñata* I promised you."

"¡Viva!" I cheered, hugging her tight. I loved the *piñatas* my friends had on their birthdays, and I had always dreamed of having one of my own. Now, my wish would come true!

Mama Rosa, who had come out to greet us, smiled at my excitement. "And we'll make *chiles rellenos* for your birthday dinner, too," she added, squeezing my shoulders with her big warm hands.

"Sí, chico," Mami said. "Didn't I tell you that if you got good grades, you would have a special dinner *and* a *piñata* for your birthday? Now, keep up the good work at school, and do what Mama Rosa says." Then she kissed her mother good-bye and left.

"Be careful at the border!" Mama Rosa called to Mami as she disappeared down the road.

Monday through Friday, Mami worked in Juárez's twin city, El Paso. She would catch a ride in a van with other women who, like her, worked as maids and nannies there. At the American border, she would tell the guard the same story: She was crossing the border to go shopping. She thought that being all dressed up made her story more believable. As soon as she was in El Paso, she would get on a bus for the long ride to the city's east side. Then she would get off the bus and walk the rest of the way to her final destination. Many other women lived all week in the houses where they worked. They would only return to their families on weekends. My mother was not one of them. She came home every evening to make dinner for us, to mend our clothing, and to check if I had done my homework. And I was glad to have her with me every night.

When it was time, Mama Rosa took me to school. And lucky me — to get there, we had to go by the market. In the distance I could see the vendors opening their stands and arranging their wares.

"Can we stop and look at the *piñatas* — PLEASE — Mama Rosa?" I begged.

"How many times have you seen them?" Mama Rosa laughed. But of course, she let me go.

Inside the dark market building we walked past the many stalls filled with fruits and vegetables, purses and handbags, and clothes. And then we came to the one I liked best—the big one that sold *piñatas*. Dozens of

them in all shapes and sizes hung from the ceiling. There were donkeys and horses, cats and dogs, rabbits and fish, and even a silver star. Dazzled by the brilliant colors of the tissue paper that covered them, I stared at each one, hypnotized. Then I looked in the corner to make sure my favorite one was still there — the huge red bull with multicolored ribbons tied to its horns. Standing next to him I could look right into his deep black paper eyes. He was as tall as I was. I was sure he could hold more treats than any other *piñata* there!

"Look!" I whispered to Mama Rosa. "The bull I want is still here."

"We'll see which one your Mami can buy," Mama Rosa said with a wink. "But now we must get you to school. Mami doesn't want you to be late."

"Don't worry," the vendor joked with me. "The *piñatas* will be waiting for you when you come back."

In the classroom I told my best friend Pablo about my *piñata.* He was as excited as I was. And all day long, I raised my hand to answer the teacher's questions, hoping to make the day go faster. But it went as slowly as ever.

That afternoon at Mama Rosa's I did my homework right away while I waited for Mami to return from her job. I kept thinking about my *piñata* and what we could fill it with. In the *barrio,* when someone had a *piñata,* it was hung out on the street, and all the children were invited to share in the fun. I prayed the vendor would not sell my bull before we got there.

When evening came, I sat on Mama Rosa's wooden front steps lost in my daydreams. The shadow of the saguaro cactus on the side of her house grew longer and longer until it faded into the darkness. Where was Mami? I never stayed at my grandma's this long. Would the market still be open after sunset? Behind me I heard Mama Rosa pacing in the kitchen. I was getting very hungry.

Suddenly, Papá appeared.

When he did not find us at home, he got worried and decided to come see if I was still at Mama Rosa's. Inside the house I saw them whisper to each other. Mama Rosa looked anxious as she set the table. The three of us sat down and had some *frijoles.* We ate the beans in silence.

It was late at night when Mami finally arrived. We all rose to greet her as she walked in the door. She looked frazzled.

"You won't believe the day I had!" she exclaimed.

She was out of breath. "This morning they stopped me at the border. They held me for hours, asking all kinds of questions. They asked what was I going to buy . . . how much was I going to spend . . . what stores was I going to . . . I was so nervous, I couldn't even answer. By the time they let me go, it was very late, and I thought I might lose my job. I was lucky Señora Smith didn't get mad. Then I worked late to make up for the time I lost." Mami collapsed next to me on the small couch where I sat, and her head sank into her hands. "I was careful to return after the change of border patrols," she said.

"I don't like it," Mama Rosa complained. "What if the guards filed a report? You could end up in jail. Can't you quit?"

"No," said Mami, weeping. "We need the money I bring home."

"It is true that with the money you bring we can buy many things we need," Papá said. "But it is not worth it if you get into trouble. We can do without some things."

"Like what?" Mami asked. "Roberto's school shoes? Groceries? Mama Rosa's medicine?

I rested my head on Mami's lap. It was almost midnight. She stroked my hair as she talked for a long time with Papá and Mama Rosa. Slowly their voices became fainter and fainter until they dissolved into my dreams.

The next morning, I woke up in my own bed. Papá must have carried me home. Seated at the foot of the bed Mami was singing *Las Mañanitas.* Still half asleep I realized it was my birthday.

"This evening we'll have your favorite meal," Mami said when she finished the birthday song. "Mama Rosa is coming to help me make you *chiles rellenos.*"

"*Gracias,* Mami," I whispered. I was about to ask if I was still getting my *piñata.* But when I remembered how upset Mami had been the night before, I thought it was better not to ask.

"Now get dressed, and after breakfast you'll go with Papá and help him with his errands. I need to clean the house."

I spent the morning of my birthday with Papá at the hardware store. He was buying materials he needed for a construction job. The store was close to the market, so while Papá payed, I ran to the *piñata* stand. The donkeys and the horses, the cats and the dogs, the rabbits and the fish, and the silver star dazzled more brilliantly than ever. But something was wrong. The corner where my huge bull had once stood was now empty.

My *piñata* was gone!

The burning desert sun was high when we got back home. Inside the kitchen, I found Mami roasting poblano chiles on the flat iron pan. When she finished, Mama Rosa filled them with cheese.

"Roberto," said Mami. "Go wash up and get me three, big ripe tomatoes from the garden. I need them for the *pico de gallo*."

Slowly I went out to the garden. While I was excited about my birthday dinner, I knew that without my *piñata,* my birthday wouldn't be the same.

Outside, I found Papá talking with one of our neighbors who was attaching a rope to the roof of his house. Papá leaned over a large bag and slowly removed what was inside. At first I saw a horned head appear. Then I saw a big red body.

"Papá, Papá!" I ran up to him. "It's my *piñata*! The exact one I wanted!"

"I know," he said. "Mami and Mama Rosa bought it this morning."

I started to run to get Pablo, but stopped when I heard his shout from behind me. He raced toward us, followed by about twenty other children from the *barrio*. They all lined up single file to hit my birthday *piñata* with a wooden stick. When everyone was there, Papá put a blindfold on the first child in line. All the other children watched and chanted, *"Dale, dale, dale . . ."*

By the time the bull had lost a horn and a leg, it was finally my turn. Papá blindfolded me. *"¡Dale, Roberto!"* my friends cheered. "Hit it!" I aimed high and hit the *piñata.* I heard a muffled thud and took off my blindfold to see only a single orange had fallen.

"My turn!" cried Pablo. He gave two heavy blows, and with the second one, a shower of juicy oranges, hard candy, peanuts, and sugarcane pieces came pouring down from the *piñata's* swaying shards. My *piñata* had more treats in it than any we had ever seen! Amid the laughter and shouting, all the children scrambled on the ground to pick up what they could. When I got up with my hands full, I saw Mami watching me tenderly.

The afternoon wore away, and one by one, my friends left. All except Pablo. Mama Rosa had invited him and his parents to join us for dinner. My uncles, aunt, and Pablo's parents chattered as they ate.

"Feliz cumpleaños, Roberto," Mami said as she handed me a plate with two freshly fried *chiles rellenos,* warm flour *tortillas, frijoles,* and *pico de gallo.*

"Victoria," Mama Rosa said. "Are you going back to work on Monday?"

"Sí, Mamá," Mami answered. "I have to."

"Don't you think you might get stopped again?" Mama Rosa asked anxiously.

As Pablo and I sank our teeth into the warm chiles oozing with melted cheese, Mami came to me and kissed me on the forehead. "How did you like your birthday?" she asked.

"It was the best birthday I ever had!" I answered.

Mama Rosa and Mami looked at each other, their eyes smiling with silent understanding.

"And that," Mami said, "is your answer."

The Lord of Miracles
DOÑA JOSEFA'S STORY

Many years ago on a misty October afternoon in Lima, Peru, I watched Mamá bake *turrón de Doña Pepa*. Even though she made it every year before the procession for the Lord of Miracles, I had never asked her why.

"Why do you bake *turrón* in October?" I asked. "Why is this the only time they sell it all over the city?"

"*¿Por qué, por qué?*" she sighed as she sprinkled the freshly-baked nougat with tiny colorful candies. "Always asking questions, Josefa. Why? It is because this is the month of the Lord of Miracles."

Not satisfied with her answer, I continued to ask more questions. Who was Doña Pepa? And why do so many people dress in purple around this time? Finally, I wore Mamá out and she said, "I really should tell you the beautiful story that goes with the nougat. After all, you are named after its creator, Josefina Marmanillo." Then, handing me a piece of the honey-glazed sweet, she led me to the balcony where we sat next to each

other. And as we watched the breathtaking procession down below, this is the story she told.

It all began in colonial times, when Lima was home to the Quechua Indians. It was also home to the Spanish colonists and to the *morenos,* who were brought from Africa as slaves. It was then that an old building with a thatched roof stood inside the city's stone walls. Some say it was a leprosarium. Others say it was a brotherhood of Indians and *morenos.* Yet there are those who believe that it was a barracks for African slaves. What is true, however, is that on a big adobe wall of this building, an Angolan slave had painted an unusually beautiful black image of Christ.

A few years later, in 1655, a powerful earthquake shook Lima. It demolished everything — from government palaces, mansions, and monasteries to the humblest of homes. Thousands of lives were lost to the mighty tremors. But in the wake of its destruction, survivors gathered on top of the rubble of the old building to witness a phenomenal sight. The fragile adobe wall where the *moreno* Christ had been painted stood perfectly intact!

Word of the event spread among the slaves, and the haunting image of the black Christ became a source of miracles for many. Some of the faithful are said to have been healed of incurable diseases. Others vowed to have been granted long-awaited favors. So in time, the painting became known as *el Señor de los Milagros.* By the 1700s, a church was built to house the image, and the purple-clad nuns from the convent next door became the caretakers of the shrine.

It was around this time that Josefina Marmanillo lived. Josefina was a slave woman who worked on a cotton farm in a coastal valley south of Lima. Known to all as Doña Pepa the *morena,* she spent long days in the farmhouse kitchen kneading, pounding, peeling, and slicing with her big wrinkled hands. And even in the strongest desert heat, she never failed to sing while she worked. She would stop only to laugh when one of the children of the house sneaked in to steal her scrumptious sweets.

One day, while working in the kitchen, a weakness overcame her. Later, she noticed her chores took longer to do. And soon, even the simplest task became impossible. Her cheerful laugh was silenced. And as her arms became paralyzed, her master freed her. For so many years Doña Pepa had thrived on caring for all the people that delighted in her wonderful cooking and baking. Now she was crippled.

That October, when Doña Pepa heard about *el Señor de los Milagros* and the procession that was to be held in His honor, her hopes soared, and she boarded a ship bound for the capital city. The *morena* believed that if she joined the religious caravan and followed the Christ's bier on her knees as a sacrifice to the Lord of Miracles, she might be cured.

It was a chilly day that October when the freed slave arrived in Lima. Above the city hovered the *garúa,* a damp, cold mist that blocked the sun. The city looked as mournful as the procession itself. Doña Pepa looked at the *moreno* Christ from the distance, then fell to her knees and joined the followers. She found herself surrounded by others who, like her, had placed their hopes in the Lord of Miracles. Enveloped by the soothing rhythm of continuous prayer, she accompanied the painting of Christ through long, cobblestone streets and hard dirt roads, until her long skirt was torn and her knees bled. She endured the pain for many long hours, and just as she felt she could not take any more, a tingling sensation suddenly returned to her fingertips. It crept up past her elbows, then went to her shoulders. Had her prayers been answered? Slowly, she clasped her hands together, then pinched her forearms. She could move her arms and hands again! She fell to the ground and wept, for the *moreno* Christ had heard her.

"Ay, Señor de los Milagros," she whispered. "Whatever you ask of me, I shall do."

Doña Pepa spent the next few weeks trying to think of a way she could thank the Lord of Miracles. The answer finally came to her in a dream. She dreamed of orange-blossom honey perfumed with lemons and laced with aniseed. When she woke up the next morning, she ran to her tiny kitchen and invented a luscious nougat candy. As soon as it was ready, she filled the tray with the sweet confection and rushed to the courtyard of the *moreno* Christ's shrine where the poor gathered. There, she gave nougat to each man, woman, and child. At first, she told her story to all who asked her why she did this. Then she retold it to all who would listen. It is said that every October until her death, Doña Pepa baked large trays of the golden delicacy to feed to the needy. And as she told her story, she offered them hope for a miracle of their own.

Mamá said as she finished her story, "You know, my dear Josefa, Lima has witnessed hundreds of processions for the Lord of Miracles since they started in 1687. Year after year, you've seen how hundreds of thousands of believers cloaked in purple, like the first caretakers of the *moreno* Christ, come to profess their faith. And you've seen how in the path of the procession, buildings are lavishly adorned with purple garlands of flowers. You've heard the chants and the prayers that mingle with the fragrance of incense in the dim candlelight. And you've seen the gold-and-silver bier with the painted image of *el Señor de los Milagros* that is carried through Lima's streets. But of all the gifts of song, incense, and myrrh offered to the black Christ, none compare to the humble gift of the *morena.*

"And that is why to this day, Josefa, her delicious nougat is sold on every street corner of the city. It is to remind us what true faith in the Lord of Miracles can bring."

Aguinaldo

When I was growing up in Puerto Rico, I went to a small, Catholic girls' school. Every December, Sister Antonia, our religion teacher, insisted that the sixth grade visit the nursing home in Santurce. Bringing Christmas cheer to the old and infirm was an experience she felt all sixth graders should have. But the year I was in fifth grade, Sister Antonia decided our class was mature enough to join the older girls and have that experience, too.

"I'm not going," I whispered to my friend Margarita.

"You have to, Marilia," she said. "Everyone has to go."

All of my classmates looked forward to the trip. Some, because they liked the rackety bus ride to anywhere. Some, because they could skip school for the day and that meant no homework. And others, because they believed that to do a sixth-grade activity in fifth grade was very special. But ever since my only grandma died in a nursing home, the thought of going back to one made me feel sad. I didn't want to go.

As I sat at my desk coloring the Christmas card that I was assigned to make for a resident, I tried to figure out how I could skip this field trip. Maybe they would let me help at the library. Maybe I could write a special book report at school while they were out. Or better yet, I could wake up ill and stay home from school. As soon as the recess bell rang, I ran over to the library to try out my first plan.

"*Hola,* Marilia," Señora Collazo greeted me.

"*Hola,* Señora Collazo," I said, smiling sweetly. "I came to ask you if I could stay here tomorrow to help you paint posters for the book fair. I really don't mind spending the whole day at the library."

"Aren't you going on a field trip tomorrow?" Señora Collazo asked.

"My class is going. But I could be excused if you need my help." The librarian thanked me and said that if I wanted to help I could join the other students who had already volunteered to stay after school to do the posters. Biting my lower lip, I left the library in a hurry. It was time to try my second plan.

Outside, seated on the polished tiles of the covered corridor, my friends were having a tournament of jacks. But I didn't join them. Instead, I marched right to the sixth-grade classroom. Sister Antonia was grading papers at her desk as I went in.

"Sister Antonia," I said softly.

"Yes, Marilia," Sister Antonia answered.

I stared for a moment at the buckles of my shoes. Then without looking up, I took a deep breath, swept back my black curls, and asked, "May I stay in school tomorrow to do an extra book report?"

"I'm afraid not, Marilia," Sister Antonia said firmly. "Tomorrow is our trip to the nursing home. Both the fifth and sixth grades are going. But if you want to do an extra book report, you can do it over the weekend."

I glanced across the room to the trays of *besitos de coco,* the coconut sweets that the sixth graders had prepared to bring to the nursing-home residents as an *aguinaldo. Aguinaldos,* surprise Christmas gifts, were fun to receive. But still, I wasn't going, so it wasn't my concern. I whispered thank you to the sister, and left.

That evening at dinnertime, I put my third plan into action. To my parents' surprise, I had two big helpings of rice and kidney beans, two helpings of Mami's *tembleque* for dessert, and three glasses of mango juice. I *never* ate so much. I figured that with all this food, I was sure to get indigestion. I went to bed and waited. I tossed and turned. I waited for several hours expecting a stomachache any second, but instead, the heavy meal made me tired and I fell sound asleep.

"Marilia, get dressed!" Mami called early the next morning. "We have to leave soon for school!"

How unlucky. I woke up feeling quite well. There was only one thing left to do, I ran to the bathroom, let the hot water run, and drank a full glass of it. Then I went back to bed.

"Marilia." Mami came in. "Get up! What is going on with you?"

"I feel warm, Mami," I mumbled.

Mami looked at me with concern. She touched my forehead and my neck. Then she left the room and in a few minutes came back with the thermometer in her hands. I opened my mouth and she slipped it under my tongue.

When the time was up, Mami pulled the thermometer out and read it.

"One hundred and six degrees?" she exclaimed. "That's impossible. You look perfectly fine to me."

After a little questioning, I confessed what I had done. I told Mami how much I didn't want to go on the field trip.

"You know, Marilia," she advised, "you might enjoy yourself after all. Besides, I've already promised Sister Antonia two trays of *tembleque* to bring as an *aguinaldo* to the residents of the home."

There was no way out. I had to go.

In the big lobby of the nursing home, paper streamers hung from the tall windows. The residents were scattered everywhere. Some were seated on the couches. Some were in wheelchairs. Some walked clutching onto their walkers. A nurse hovered over a group of men as she dispensed pills. Sister Antonia took out her guitar and at the sound of the first bar we began to sing a medley of carols. Several of the girls accompanied with *maracas, güiro,* and *palitos.* Meanwhile, the residents clapped and sang along while a sixth grader passed around our cards for us to give to them later. As I watched how happy our music made the residents, memories of my grandma rushed to me, making me dizzy with sadness. Suddenly, I saw that everybody was visiting with the residents. I was alone. I didn't feel like joining one of the groups. Maybe I could quietly slip away until the visit was over. I hoped it would be soon. Then I noticed a chair against the yellow wall. I sat there still holding the card I had made.

Across the room there was a frail old lady in a wheelchair. She was alone, too. I looked at my card again. It was rather pretty. I had painted it with shades of blue and gold. Maybe I could just hand it to her and leave. It might brighten her day. So gingerly, I crossed the lobby and stood next to her.

"Who is there?" the old lady asked as she coquettishly fixed her silver bun with the light touch of her manicured hand.

"My name is Marilia," I said. "I brought you a card."

"Dios te bendiga," the old woman said. "God bless you."

She reached for the card but her hand was nowhere near it. Her gaze was lost in the distance, and I knelt down to place the card in her hand. It was then that I saw the big clouds in her eyes. She was blind. *What was the use of a card if you couldn't see it?* I felt cheated. I stood up to go back to my chair.

"My name is Elenita," she said as I tried to slip away. "Tell me, Marilia, what does your card look like?"

I knelt down beside her and, in as vivid detail as I could, described the three wise men I had drawn. Then, Elenita's curious fingers caressed every inch of the card. She couldn't have enjoyed it more if she had seen it.

When the coconut sweets were passed around, she mischievously asked for two.

"I bet you are not supposed to eat one of these," she giggled.

"No," I replied. "Sister Antonia told us that the sweets were just for residents."

"Well," she whispered. "Nobody said I couldn't give you one of *mine*."

67

I liked Elenita. I placed the *besito de coco* in my mouth and relished it even more. Especially since I wasn't supposed to have it. I enjoyed being her partner in mischief. After that, she asked me if I liked music and if I knew how do dance.

"Ay," I said, "I love to listen to music and dance."

Then she told me how, when she was young, she had been a great dancer.

"I used to dance so well that men would line up for a chance to dance with me. I had many, many suitors at one time," she said. "I had suitors that serenaded me in the evening and others that brought me flowers. But I didn't go out with all of them. You have to be selective, you know."

Too soon we were interrupted by Sister Antonia. It was time to get on the bus and return to school. I didn't want to leave.

"Thank you for the card, Marilia," Elenita said. She opened her hand and gestured for me to give her mine. "I'll keep this card to remember you by."

"I'm sorry you can't see it," I said as I squeezed her hand. For a moment it felt as warm and giving as my own grandma's. "I wished I had brought you a better *aguinaldo*."

"The best *aguinaldo*," Elenita said, "was your visit, Marilia."

As I left, I felt light and warm and peaceful. On the bus ride back, I told my friend Margarita all about our visit. I couldn't wait to come back next year when I was in the sixth grade. I already knew what I would bring Elenita. I would make her a collage. That way she would be able to feel the many textures of my picture, even if she couldn't see it. And maybe I could make the picture of her dancing. I knew she had been very pretty when she was young.

"Are you going to wait until next Christmas to give her your collage?" Margarita asked.

I thought for a moment. "Maybe Mami could bring me back sooner," I said.

As I looked out the window, I remembered how good Elenita's hand felt to touch. It's funny how sometimes things change unexpectedly. Just that morning I didn't want to go at all. But then, I couldn't wait to visit my new friend again. We had gone to the nursing home to give *aguinaldos.* And what a very special *aguinaldo* I had been given — Elenita's friendship.

Carmen Teresa's Gift

"*¡Bueno!*" cheers Abuelito from the head of the table after the last story had been told. "Wonderful stories, all of them!"

"*¡Sí!* Oh, yes!" a chorus of voices answer Abuelito from around the room. "Wonderful stories."

Abuelito looks pleased. "Now tell us, Carmen Teresa, which of the stories will you write down first?"

I am about to answer, but everyone answers for me.

"She will record the stories in the order she heard them," Mamá says. "It's the only fair way."

"*No, no,*" says Abuelita. "There are too many. She should write only the ones she likes best."

"I saw Carmen Teresa laughing while I told my story," Abita confides in Abuelita. "I'll bet she will choose mine." Abuelita nods in agreement.

Uncle Robert thinks I should write down everything I can remember. Tía Marilia generously offers to write hers. "It will make it easier for you," she assures me.

Suddenly, Flor appears from the kitchen with another tray of *natilla* and *flan de coco.* After everyone has taken seconds, she whispers to me that her story doesn't have to be included if there isn't room. But I can tell that she hopes there is.

"Carmen Teresa!" my sister Laura calls from across the table. She has already finished Alex's and her *natilla* and licks her spoon clean before she reaches for a third helping. But Mamá stops her.

"After you write those stories down in your book," Laura says sweetly, "I'll draw pictures to go along with them."

"Now, there is a fine idea!" says Abuelo Jaime. "You two can work on the book together."

By now, everyone has told me what they think I should do with my gift. Most of the children are no longer interested in the discussion and flee to the basement to play. Just as I am about to join the kids downstairs, Abuelito's deep voice stops me.

"Carmen Teresa!" he commands. "Let's get started right away. Sit next to me and we'll write my story together. Laura, you can start drawing the pictures."

"No." My voice comes out louder than I intend it to.

Instantly, the room becomes silent.

"Carmen Teresa!" Mamá scolds.

"Why don't we let Carmen Teresa decide for herself what she wants to do with her gift," Doña Josefa suggests. "After all, the present was meant for her."

Everyone eagerly waits for me to speak. I know exactly what I want to do. I hug the blank book, and look at each one of the relatives and friends around me. Then I begin.

"In all of your stories, you all mentioned some kind of special food. I want to collect the recipes for all the foods you told about in my book. And I will add the recipes for the foods Mamá served here today."

"That is a delightful idea, Carmen Teresa," says Doña Josefa.

"Yes," agrees Abuelito, "and Abuelita can finally tell you how to make *tortilla española.*" He laughs as he squeezes Abuelita's hand. "She's taken all these years to learn how to make it just like Mami used to."

"I could also give you José Manuel's recipe for *surullitos,*" adds Abuelita. "It's as good as his grandmother's."

"But the best recipe for *alfajores argentinos,*" boasts Abita, "is the one I make."

As everyone chatters merrily about their recipes, Doña Josefa talks to me alone.

"I'm so pleased you liked my gift, Carmen Teresa," she says. "Each time you prepare one of these recipes, you will remember the story that was told with it. And each time someone tastes one of these dishes, they, too, might have a story to tell."

Content that I have finally found a way to make this

present my very own, I borrow Doña Josefa's fountain pen and open my book to the first page. Then, with great flourishes and curls, I write:

Carmen Teresa's Book of Fantastic Family Recipes

Gently, I blow on the wet ink to dry it, and I close the book. And tomorrow, I will begin collecting my recipes.

Carmen Teresa's Book of ~ Fantastic Family Recipes

Mamá's Arroz con Pollo
CHICKEN WITH RICE
PUERTO RICO

2½ lbs. skinless chicken thighs

juice of 2 limes

Adobo *seasoning**

1 oz. salt pork, diced

2 oz. cured ham, diced

2 tbs. olive oil

4 garlic cloves, peeled and crushed

1 lg. onion, peeled and chopped

2 lg. green peppers, seeded and chopped

1 tomato, chopped

pimento-stuffed Spanish olives

capers

3 cups long grain rice

3½ cups water

1½ cubes chicken bouillon

¼ cup tomato paste

2 envelopes Sazón *seasoning**

½ cup fresh cilantro, chopped

salt and pepper

*Available where Latin foods are sold

Coat the chicken with lime juice and sprinkle generously with Adobo seasoning. Set in refrigerator overnight.

In a *caldero,* a heavy pot, brown the pork and ham in olive oil over medium-high heat. Add garlic and marinated chicken. Reduce heat to moderate. Brown the chicken for 5 to 10 minutes then remove the chicken pieces and set them aside. Add onion, green peppers, and tomato to the pot, and sauté until tender. Replace the chicken, and add olives and capers to taste. Add rice, water, chicken bouillon cubes, tomato paste, Sazón seasoning, cilantro, and salt and pepper to taste. Stir well. Cover and bring to a boil. Then turn heat to low and cook for 20 minutes. Turn rice with a wooden spoon. Keep covered on the stove with the heat off for 10 to 15 minutes more.   *Serves 6 to 8.*

Have an adult help you when frying or boiling.

Mamá's Yuca con Mojo Criollo
STEAMED YUCA WITH SAUCE
PUERTO RICO

YUCA

2½ lbs. frozen yuca (also called
   cassava)*

water

salt

juice of one lemon

mojo criollo *sauce*
   (see recipe below)

*Available where Latin foods are sold

Place frozen yuca in a large pot. Cover with water and sprinkle with salt. Boil for at least 1 hour. Meanwhile, prepare *mojo criollo.*

When the yuca is very tender, remove it from the water with a slotted spoon, and arrange on a platter. Sprinkle with lemon juice, salt to taste, and pour *mojo criollo* on top. Serve immediately.

Mojo Criollo Sauce

4 lg. onions, peeled and sliced

6 garlic cloves, peeled and sliced

1 cup olive oil

4 bay leaves

1 tsp. peppercorns

In a large saucepan, sauté onions and garlic in olive oil until the onions are soft, but still white. Add bay leaves and peppercorns, and simmer covered for ½ hour.

Serves 8.

Have an adult help you when frying or boiling.

Flor's Bacalao a la Vizcaína

CODFISH STEW

GUATEMALA

1 lb. dried, salted codfish fillets*

water

One 6-oz. can tomato paste

½ cup olive oil

¼ cup pimento-stuffed Spanish olives

1 tbs. capers

2 garlic cloves, peeled and crushed

1 bay leaf

4 medium potatoes,
  peeled and thinly sliced

2 medium onions, peeled and thinly
  sliced

*Available where Latin foods are sold

Cover codfish in water and soak for 4 hours, changing the water twice. Drain well. Place codfish in a pot with 8 cups of water, and boil for 15 minutes. Drain and let cool. Discard skin and bones, and then shred the flesh.

Mix tomato paste with 1 cup water and olive oil, and stir until paste is smooth. Add olives, capers, garlic, and bay leaf to the tomato mixture.

In a large frying pan, arrange alternate layers of tomato mixture, potatoes, codfish, and onions. Bring to a boil over medium-high heat and cover. Turn heat to low, and cook for 30 minutes or until potatoes are tender. Transfer to serving platter.

Serves 4 to 6.

Have an adult help you when frying or boiling.

Flor's Torrejas
GUATEMALAN TOAST

GUATEMALA

TOAST

½ lb. French bread

1 cup milk

ground cinnamon to taste

3 eggs, lightly beaten

vegetable oil, for panfrying

To prepare *torrejas,* cut bread into ½-inch-thick slices. Dip each slice in milk. Remove with a slotted spoon and place on a cookie sheet. Sprinkle both sides of the bread with cinnamon. Dip into beaten eggs and remove with a slotted spoon. Fry bread slices in hot oil until both sides are golden brown. Remove. Drain on absorbent paper towels and place several slices in each dessert bowl. Serve with syrup *(see recipe below)*.

SYRUP

2 cups sugar

1 cup water

¼ tsp. salt

1 thin cinnamon stick

peel of 1 lime, grated

For the syrup, mix sugar, water, salt, cinnamon stick, and lime peel in a saucepan. Boil over high heat without stirring until syrup thickens slightly, about 20 minutes. Pour syrup over toast. Allow the syrup to cool a little before serving. Enjoy *torrejas* with a tall glass of milk. *Serves 4.*

Have an adult help you when frying or boiling.

Flor's Horchata

SESAME DRINK

GUATEMALA

1 cup sesame seeds

6 cups water

½ cup sugar

ice

Soak sesame seeds in 4 cups of water for 3 hours. Drain well. Crush seeds in a food processor or with a mortar. Add seeds to 2 cups of lukewarm water, mix, and squeeze mixture through a muslin cloth into a pot. Add sugar, mix, and refrigerate to chill. Stir well. Serve in a tall glass with ice. *Serves 4.*

Fernando's Tortilla Española

SPANISH OMELET

C U B A

¼ cup olive oil

1 lg. onion, peeled and chopped

1¼ tsp. salt

1 Spanish chorizo*, skinless and
   minced (optional)

1 lb. new potatoes, washed and cut in
   small irregular shapes

6 lg. eggs

⅛ tsp. ground pepper

*Available where Latin foods are sold

Place oil, onion, ¼ tsp. salt, and *chorizo* (optional) in a 10-inch nonstick frying pan. Sauté for 10 minutes over low heat, stirring occasionally. Strain in a colander, reserving oil. Set onions aside and pour oil back into pan. Add potatoes and ¼ tsp. salt. Turn heat to high, then when mixture sizzles, cover and cook over low heat until potatoes are tender, about 25 minutes. Remove potatoes with a slotted spoon and set aside.

In a bowl, beat eggs with the pepper and ¾ tsp. salt. Stir in onions and potatoes. Turn heat to medium-high. Pour egg mixture into frying pan. Cook over medium-high heat for 2 to 3 minutes, then turn heat to low. Cook *tortilla* until surface is dry. Gently move pan back and forth to release the edges of the *tortilla*. Then, put a plate over the top of the pan. Using oven mitts, turn the pan over onto the plate. Once the *tortilla* is on the plate, slip it back into the pan to cook for 10 minutes on the other side. Remove from the pan and let cool before cutting into 1½-inch cubes. Serve at room temperature.   *Makes about 32 appetizers.*

Have an adult help you when frying.

Amalia's Helado de Coco

COCONUT SHERBET

PUERTO RICO

One 14-oz. can unsweetened coconut milk

1½ cups sugar

⅛ tsp. salt

3½ cups water

peel of ⅛ lime, grated

Mix all ingredients well. Pour in a freezer container and freeze for several hours until the sherbet is half frozen. Remove from freezer and beat the sherbet to break up crystals. For a smoother texture, you can repeat this process. Freeze overnight or until firm.

Serves 10 to 12.

José Manuel's Surullitos de Maíz

CORN FRITTERS

PUERTO RICO

CORN FRITTERS

2 cups water

1¼ tsp. salt

1½ cups yellow cornmeal

1 cup grated Edam or Colby cheese

vegetable oil for deep-frying

Combine water and salt in a saucepan. Heat to boiling and remove from heat. Add cornmeal and mix thoroughly. Cook over moderate heat for about 10 minutes or until mixture separates from the bottom and sides of pan. Mixture will be thick and steam will rise from it. Remove from heat. Add cheese and mix well. Let cool slightly. Take mixture by the tablespoon, and roll it in the palms of your hands to form ½-inch-thick cylinders with rounded ends. Deep-fry in oil heated to 375° F. until golden brown. Remove and drain on absorbent paper. Serve warm with salsa.

Makes about 50.

Have an adult help you when frying.

SALSA

½ cup mayonnaise

½ cup ketchup

3 peeled garlic cloves, crushed

Mix all ingredients together and serve as a cold dip for the warm *surullitos.*

88

Susana's Alfajores

CARAMEL SANDWICH COOKIES

ARGENTINA

1 1/3 cup cornstarch

3/4 cup and 3 tbs. all-purpose flour

1/2 tsp. baking soda

2 tsp. baking powder

7 oz. butter, softened

1/2 cup and 3 tbs. sugar

3 egg yolks

peel of 1 lemon, grated

1 tsp. vanilla

dulce de leche *(see recipe below)*

powdered sugar

Preheat oven to 350° F. In small bowl, mix cornstarch, flour, baking soda, and baking powder. Set aside. In a food processor, mix butter with sugar. Mix in egg yolks, one by one. Add flour mixture by spoonfuls, mixing well after each addition. Finally, add lemon peel and vanilla. Mix well. Scrape sides of bowl and transfer the dough onto a floured surface. If dough is too soft, chill until easier to handle. With a floured rolling pin, roll the dough out to a ¼-inch thickness. Or, roll between two sheets of waxed paper. With a cookie cutter, make 2-inch diameter rounds. Place rounds on a cookie sheet. Bake for 10 minutes or until pale golden-brown. Let cookies cool. Make cookie sandwiches using *dulce de leche* as a filling. Sift a generous amount of powdered sugar on top of *alfajores.*   *Makes about 16.*

Dulce de Leche

One 14-oz. can sweetened condensed milk   1 tsp. vanilla

Place unopened can of sweetened condensed milk in a deep pan. Cover can with water. Bring to a boil. Boil for 2 hours, keeping the can under water at all times. Remove from pan. Let it cool completely. Open can and pour its contents into a small bowl. Stir in vanilla.   *Makes enough filling for 16 alfajores.*

Have an adult help you remove the can from boiling water.

Mama Rosa's Chiles Rellenos

STUFFED FRIED PEPPERS

M E X I C O

12 cubanel or poblano peppers

Monterey Jack cheese, sliced into thick rectangular pieces

3 lg. eggs, whites and yolks separated

oil for deep-frying

In a *comal,* a heavy iron pan, roast peppers on all sides until the skin turns brown-black and begins to lift. Remove peppers from pan with tongs. While peppers are still warm, carefully peel off their skins. Make a 2-inch slit in each one and remove the seeds with a small spoon. Stuff each pepper with a piece of cheese. Set aside.

In a large bowl, beat egg whites until stiff. Gently fold in egg yolks. Dip peppers in beaten egg mixture and fry in hot oil. When peppers turn golden brown, remove with a slotted spoon and serve immediately. Enjoy *chiles rellenos* with *pico de gallo.*

Serves 12.

Have an adult help you when frying.

Victoria's Flour Tortillas

MEXICAN PANCAKES

4½ cups all-purpose flour

1 tsp. salt

3½ tbs. canola oil

1 cup lukewarm water

In a large bowl, mix flour and salt. Cut in oil with a fork until mixture resembles coarse meal. Add water gradually and knead until dough forms a large ball. It should be elastic, but not sticky. Cover the ball with a towel for ½ hour.

Pinch off disks of dough 1 inch thick and 2 inches in diameter. Roll each one into a flat, thin circle. Heat a heavy iron pan until a drop of water sizzles in it. Cook *tortillas* until both sides are golden brown. Enjoy with meat filling, *pico de gallo,* shredded cheese, or by themselves.

Makes about 28.

Roberto's Pico de Gallo

MEXICAN RELISH

2 lg. ripe tomatoes, chopped

1 lg. onion, peeled and chopped

1 bunch of cilantro, stalks removed,
leaves rinsed and chopped

1 jalapeño pepper, seeded and finely
chopped

juice of 2 limes

Mix all ingredients together in a large bowl. Serve with warm flour *tortillas.*

Josefa's Turrón de Doña Pepa
NOUGAT CANDY
PERU

DOUGH

2½ cups all-purpose flour

2 tsp. baking powder

1 tbs. aniseed

4 egg yolks

8 oz. butter

¼ cup aniseed herbal tea

1 tsp. salt

¼ cup milk

Preheat oven to 350° F. Mix flour, baking powder, and aniseed in a bowl. In another bowl, beat egg yolks. Add beaten egg yolks to flour mixture. Cut in butter with your hands until mixture resembles cornmeal. In a third bowl, mix aniseed tea, salt, and milk. Add this liquid mixture to the flour-and-egg mixture. Knead until you can form a ball with the dough. Let dough stand at room temperature for 1 hour.

Roll dough to form long cylinders ¼-inch thick. Cut into

4-inch lengths. Place the cylinder cookies on a greased cookie sheet and bake for about 20 minutes or until golden brown. Remove from oven and let cool.

Have an adult help you when baking.

HONEY

16 oz. Panela* (Hard brown sugar)	peel of ½ orange, grated
½ cup water	1 cinnamon stick
2 cloves	juice of ½ lime
juice of 1 lemon	*Available where Latin foods are sold

Place all ingredients except the lime juice in a saucepan over medium heat. Carefully stir until *Panela* melts and the liquid becomes the consistency of honey, about 20 minutes. Add lime juice so mixture doesn't crystallize. Let cool.

ASSEMBLY

For the assembly, have your favorite sugar sprinkles on hand. When the honey has cooled to the point that it will stick to the cylinder-shaped cookies, arrange alternate layers of cookies and honey in a 9- by 13-inch dish. The cookies should be layered in a crisscross fashion and the last layer should be honey. Top with sprinkles or any kind of tiny, hard-candy pieces.

As soon as the *turrón* is completely cool, cut into small pieces.

Makes about 25 pieces.

Marilia's Besitos de Coco

COCONUT KISSES

PUERTO RICO

3¼ cups fresh frozen grated coconut,*
firmly packed

1 cup brown sugar, firmly packed

8 tbs. all-purpose flour

¼ tsp. salt

4 tbs. butter, at room temperature

3 lg. egg yolks

½ tsp. vanilla

  *Available where Latin foods are sold

Preheat oven to 350° F. Place grated coconut in a bowl. Add brown sugar, flour, salt, butter, yolks, and vanilla. Mix well. Grease a 9- by 13-inch glass baking dish. Take mixture by the tablespoon, shape into balls, and arrange in baking dish. Bake for about 35 minutes or until golden. Let cool in baking dish for 10 minutes. With a small spatula, remove *besitos* carefully and place upside down onto platter. Let cool completely and turn over.

Makes about 35.

Marilia's Tembleque

COCONUT DESSERT

PUERTO RICO

¾ cup sweetened coconut milk (shake
   can before measuring)

1½ cups water

½ cup cornstarch

¾ cup milk

¼ tsp. salt

cinnamon to taste

In a large bowl, mix together all ingredients except cinnamon. Pour mixture into a large pot. Place pot over medium-high heat. Stir constantly with a wooden spoon. When mixture begins to thicken, turn heat to low and stir until it is very thick and smooth, about 10 minutes. You should be able to see the bottom of the pan when running the spoon across it.

Spread mixture into a 9- by 13-inch glass baking dish. With a fork, draw swirls on top of the *tembleque.* Sprinkle with cinnamon. Let cool. Cover and refrigerate for several hours. Once *tembleque* is chilled, it should have the consistency of gelatin. Cut into squares and transfer to a serving platter.

Makes about 30 squares.

Abuelita's Natilla

CUSTARD

PUERTO RICO

4 egg yolks

¾ cup sugar

¼ tsp. salt

2 tbs. cornstarch

4 cups whole milk

2 tsp. vanilla

ground cinnamon

Using an electric hand mixer, beat the egg yolks in a large bowl. Continue beating and add sugar slowly. Mix in salt and corn-starch until ingredients are evenly distributed and you have a smooth mixture. Set aside.

Heat the milk in a large saucepan over medium heat. It should not boil. Transfer the milk into a glass measuring cup. Pour heated milk in a steady stream over the egg yolk mixture. Beat at low speed. Transfer the mixture into a large pot and place it over medium-high heat. Stir constantly with a wooden spoon. Once the mixture starts bubbling, turn heat to low and simmer until cream thickens, about 15 minutes. It should have the consistency of thick, chocolate syrup. Remove from heat and stir in vanilla. Pour into small bowls. Sprinkle generously with cinnamon. Once the *natilla* cools completely, cover bowls and refrigerate until cold.

Serves 4 to 6.

Mamá's Flan de Coco
COCONUT FLAN
PUERTO RICO

1 cup sugar	*One 15-oz. can sweetened coconut milk*
One 14-oz. can sweetened condensed milk	*6 large eggs*
One 12-oz. can evaporated milk	

Preheat oven to 350° F. Place sugar in a 9-inch fluted tube pan. Place the pan on the stove top over medium-high heat. Sugar will dissolve and turn caramel brown. After it has melted, wear oven mitts and gently rock the pan so that the bottom and sides become coated with caramel. The caramel does not have to reach the rim. Set aside.

Place condensed milk, evaporated milk, coconut milk, and eggs in a large bowl. Using an electric hand mixer, beat at medium speed until mixture is smooth. Pour into the caramelized pan.

The flan has to cook in a boiling-water bath. Pour water to cover the bottom of a deep pan that is larger than the tube pan.

The water has to be at least 1 inch deep. Place the filled tube pan in the water. Place both pans in oven. Cook for one hour or until a toothpick comes out clean. Take tube pan out of the water and remove from oven. Let flan cool completely. With a knife, gently loosen sides of flan. Turn flan over onto a large round platter and pour the caramel syrup remaining in the tube pan on top of the flan. *Serves 12 to 14.*

Have an adult help you caramelize the pan.

A Note from the Author
ABOUT THE RECIPES

The country mentioned before each recipe is meant to show where that particular variation of the recipe comes from. However, most of these recipes are popular in many other Spanish-speaking countries in addition to the country mentioned. For example, it is well known that *flan* is a common dessert in Spain, Mexico, Peru, Ecuador, Costa Rica, and Argentina, among others. But the coconut-flavored variation of *flan* is more specific to Puerto Rico. Perhaps it is less known that the flour *tortilla*, which is frequently associated with Mexico, is also a staple food of Guatemala, El Salvador, and Costa Rica.

All the recipes included have been tested in my kitchen. Many have been favorites of my family for generations.

Glossary

ABUELA (ah-BWEH-lah): Grandmother

ABUELITA (ah-bweh-LEE-tah): Grandmother (*Abuelita* is the diminutive term for *Abuela*)

ABUELITO (ah-bweh-LEE-toh): Grandfather (*Abuelito* is the diminutive term for *Abuelo*)

ABUELO (ah-BWEH-loh): Grandfather

AGUINALDO (ah-gee-NAHL-doh): A small Christmas present

ALFAJORES DE DULCE DE LECHE (ahl-fah-HOR-ays day DOOL-say day LEH-chay): Sandwich cookies filled with milk caramel

ALFOMBRA (ahl-FOHM-brah): A carpet or rug

APÚRATE (ah-POO-rah-tay): Hurry up

ARROZ CON POLLO (ah-RROSS kohn POH-lyoh): Rice dish with chicken

¡AY! (EYE): Oh!; used to express an emotion, such as surprise or pain

AY, SANTO DIOS (EYE, SAN-toh DEE-ohs): Oh, Dear God

BACALAO A LA VIZCAÍNA (bah-kah-LAH-oh ah lah viz-kah-EE-nah): A traditional codfish stew eaten during Lent

BARRIO (BAH-ree-oh): District or quarter

BENDITO (ben-DEE-toh): Blessed; dear

BESITOS DE COCO (beh-SEE-tohs day KOH-koh): Coconut kisses, a dessert

¡BUENO! (BWEH-noh): Good!

CALDERO (cal-DEH-roh): A small cauldron

CHICO (CHEE-koh): Little boy

CHILES RELLENOS (CHEE-lays reh-LYEH-nohs): Roasted chili peppers that are stuffed with white cheese, then coated with a beaten egg mixture and fried

CHORIZO (choh-REE-zoh): A spicy Spanish sausage

COBITOS (koh-BEE-tohs): Small hermit crabs

COMAL (koh-MAHL): A heavy iron pan

CONGRÍ (kohn-GREE): Cuban rice with black beans

COQUITO (koh-KEE-toh): Holiday drink made with coconut milk and rum

CUCURUCHO DE MANÍ (koo-koo-ROO-choh day mah-NEE): A paper cone of roasted peanuts

Los Cucuruchos (los koo-koo-ROO-chohs): The porters

Cuentos (KWEN-tohs): Stories

¡Cuidado! (kwee-DAH-doh): Careful! Look out!

¡Dale! (DAH-lay): Hit it!

Damas primero (DAH-mahs pree-MEH-roh): Ladies first

Dame un beso (Dah-may oon BEH-soh): Give me a kiss

Dios te bendiga (dee-OHS tay ben-DEE-gah): God bless you

Doña (DOH-nyah): Title of courtesy and respect preceding a woman's first name

Feliz año nuevo (feh-LEEZ AH-nyoh NWEH-voh): Happy New Year

Feliz cumpleaños (feh-LEEZ koom-play-AH-nyohs): Happy birthday

Flan de coco (FLAN day KOH-koh): Coconut custard made with milk, sugar, and eggs

Frijoles (free-HOH-lays): Beans

Garúa (gah-ROO-ah): Drizzle

Gracias (GRAH-see-ahs): Thank you

Güiro (GWEE-roh): A percussion instrument played by scraping a stick along the notched surface of a gourd

Helado de coco (ay-LAH-doh day KOH-koh): Coconut-flavored sherbet

Hola (OH-lah): Hello

La hora del té (lah OH-rah del TAY): Teatime

Horchata (or-CHAH-tah): A chilled drink made of sugar, water, and crushed sesame seeds

Mamá (mah-MAH): Mama

Maraca (mah-RAH-kah): A rattle; a percussion instrument played by shaking a gourd filled with dry beans or small stones

M'ijo (MEE-hoh): Shortened form of mi hijo, which means "my son"

Mojo criollo (MOH-hoh cree-OH-lyoh): A sauce made with onion, garlic, olive oil, bay leaves, and peppercorns

Morenos (moh-RAY-nohs): Africans brought to Peru as slaves (moreno is the singular, masculine form and morena is the singular, feminine)

¡Muy peligroso! (MWEE peh-lee-GROH-soh): Too dangerous!

Nada (NAH-dah): Nothing

Natilla (nah-TEE-lyah): A creamy custard made with sugar, milk, egg yolks, and vanilla

Niña (NEE-nyah): Small girl

¡Niños! (NEE-nyohs): Children!

Palitos (pah-LEE-tohs): Sticks used to make sound by striking them against each other

Pico de gallo (PEE-koh day GAH-lyoh): Relish made with tomato, onion, cilantro, and jalapeño peppers

Piñata (pee-NYAH-tah): A decorated vessel, usually made of

papier-mâché, that is filled with fruit, candy, and peanuts

¿Por qué? (por KAY): Why?

¡Qué mala pata! (kay MAH-lah PAH-tah): What bad luck!

Querida (keh-REE-dah): Darling or dear

Salsa (SAHL-sah): A style of Latin American music and dance; also, any kind of sauce

¡Salud, dinero, amor, y tiempo para disfrutarlos! (sah-LOOD, dee-NEH-roh, ah-MORE, ee tee-EHM-poh pah-rah dis-froo-TAHR-lohs): Health, money, love, and time to enjoy it all

Señor (say-NYOR): Mister or sir

El Señor de los Milagros (el say-NYOR day los mee-LAH-gross): Lord of Miracles

Señora (say-NYOR-ah): Missus

Sí (SEE): Yes

¡Sinvergüenza! (sin-vair-GWEHN-zah): Little rascal!

Sofrito (soh-FREE-toh): A seasoning sauce

Surullito de maíz (soo-roo-LYEE-toh day mah-YEES): Puerto Rican corn fritters

Tembleque (tem-BLEH-kay): A sweet dessert made with coconut milk

Tía (TEE-ah): Aunt

Tío (TEE-oh): Uncle

Torrejas (tor-RAY-hahs): Bread dipped in milk and egg that is pan-fried and served with homemade syrup

Tortilla (tor-TEE-lyah): A thin round cake of cornmeal or wheat flour

Tortilla española (tor-TEE-lyah ehs-pah-NYOH-lah): Potato omelet

Turrón (too-RROHN): A nougat dessert

¡Vendo yuca, plátanos, tomates! (VEN-doh YOO-kah PLAH-tah-nohs toh-MAH-tehs): Yuca, plaintains, tomatoes for sale!

¡Viva! (VEE-vah): Hurrah!

Yuca (YOO-kah): A fleshy rootstock plant; also called cassava

Acknowledgments

Many people inspired and guided me through the making of this book.

I'm very grateful to Roger Alexander Sandoval and José Rodolfo Rosales for their generous insight into Guatemalan traditions. I owe the pictorial information of Holy Week in Guatemala to my good friend Germán Oliver.

Rodolfo Perez and Lucía González shared their memories of growing up in Cuba. Olga Alonso shared not only her childhood anecdotes, but also her recipes. Thank you.

I also thank Iris Brown for shedding light onto the daily life of Old San Juan in the 1940s.

For her stories about her childhood in Buenos Aires, her constant encouragement, and for instilling in me a love of cooking, I must thank my mother, Marta Orzábal de Delacre. Nellie Carpio was a great help in the search for the perfect recipe for *alfajores*.

I will not forget my Mexican friend Victoria, whose inner strength I so admire and with whom I learned how to make *chiles rellenos* and *pico de gallo*.

It was Mayté Canto who introduced me to her Peruvian friend María Rosa Watson. María Rosa's enthusiasm for the legend and traditions associated with *El Señor de los Milagros* was irresistible. To her I owe the recipe for *turrón de Doña Pepa*.

I'm greatly indebted to Diana Oliver, who was so generous to share her wonderful recipes for *tembleque, flan de coco,* and *natilla*.

I thank Priya Nair and Monique Stephens for their great assistance with back matter. I also appreciate the valuable art direction of Marijka Kostiw, Dave Caplan, and David Saylor. For her editorial direction, dedication, insight, and commitment to my work, I thank my editor, Dianne Hess.

Finally, for their unconditional love, I should thank my husband, Arturo Betancourt, and my two daughters Verónica and Alicia. Thank you, Verónica, for critiquing my stories.